SNOW DAY

By Marcia Thornton Jones and Debbie Dadey

Illustrated by Amy Wummer

Hyperion Books for Children
New York

To Ryan Nicholas Dadey for a life of happiness
and joy.   —D.D.

To Debbie Dadey—a true friend in any storm.
                                       —M.T.J.

Printed in the United States of America
First Edition
1 3 5 7 9 10 8 6 4 2
Book design by Dawn Adelman
This book is set in 14-pt. Cheltenham.
ISBN 0-7868-1551-5
Visit www.barkleyschool.com

Contents

SNOW DIAMONDS

"This is not good," my friend Woodrow said as a white flake landed on his nose and a gust of wind blew back his droopy ears. Being a basset hound, his ears were always droopy, but today his tail was drooping, too. "Not good at all."

"What is this stuff?" Bubba asked. Bubba tried to bite a flake, but missed.

I wagged my tail. Being older gave me the advantage over my little pup friend Bubba. It also helped that I was a Wonder Dog.

"This," I said with all the wisdom of my two years of life, "is snow."

Bubba, Woodrow, and I watched snow twirl around the playground of Barkley's School for Dogs. The grass sparkled with snow diamonds. Don't get me wrong. I would much rather be watching the snowfall from my apartment window with my human, Maggie. But Maggie had this idea that school would teach me to be even better than I already was.

Barkley's School for Dogs wasn't such a bad place to be. The human named Fred Barkley made sure there was plenty to do. The play yard was filled with tunnels to dash through, a teeter-totter to balance on, and bars to jump over.

"It's beautiful," Bubba whispered. "Will the snow break if we walk on it?"

I laughed. "Are you kidding? Watch this." I took a flying leap across the yard and slid on my shaggy tail a good three feet. My ears flew out behind me as I zipped along.

Bubba raced across the frozen ground and slid on his furry behind. "Growl-ific!" he shouted.

"Dog-awesome!" said my buddy, a beagle named Floyd. He ran up behind Bubba. "That looks like fun."

"It seems dangerous to me," Blondie said, trotting up beside Floyd. Blondie was the most beautiful white poodle I'd ever hope to lay my eyeballs on. Her white coat almost disappeared into the snow. I guess that's why her human had given her a blue sweater with black fur around the neck.

A little Chihuahua named Casanova trotted under my belly. "Slip-sliding in snow is bad. Very bad," he said. I looked between my legs and noticed that Casanova was bundled in a yellow sweater.

Even Bubba had on a sweater today. It was bright red against his black-and-brown chubby puppy body. Floyd had on a sweater too. I shook my head in disgust.

I looked around the yard. Rhett and Scarlett, two Irish setters, wore matching purple coats. Harry, a Westie, would have blended in with the snow if it hadn't been for his polka-dotted sweater. In fact, besides me, Woodrow was the only other dog that wasn't dressed for snow.

Woodrow was the oldest hound at Barkley's. He was also the smartest. The fact that he didn't have on a coat proved I didn't need one.

"It's not that cold out here," I teased my friends. "We're dogs. We already have built-in coats."

"My human made me wear it. It's not my fault," Bubba said before sliding across the playground on his hind end again. "Yip-pee!"

"I wouldn't mind wearing a sweater or two," Woodrow said through chattering teeth. "It's colder out here than the freezer at the ice-cream shop, and it's getting even colder. I warned you this was going to be bad."

"I'm glad my human dressed me for winter," Floyd said. "I'll stay warm enough to let me try this sliding stuff."

Floyd ran across the play yard. His paws slid out from under him and he landed on his chin. He slid right into the brick wall, nose first. "Ouch!" he yelped.

"Are you all right?" Blondie said, rushing up beside Floyd.

Floyd nodded weakly. "I've had enough fun for one day. I think I need something to chew on." Floyd almost always had a chew toy in his mouth.

"Not me," Bubba yipped and caught a few snowflakes in his mouth. He laughed when they melted. "I think snow is better than chew toys. It's better than yum-yums. It's better than bouncy balls! I wish it would snow, snow, and snow some more. Enough to cover every square inch of Barkley's School for Dogs!"

Woodrow stopped Bubba's yapping. "Be careful what you wish for," Woodrow warned. "You just might get it!"

OUT OF CONTROL

A long shadow fell over my friends and me, and the air felt even icier. We looked up into the snarling face of Sweetcakes, the meanest Doberman pinscher this side of the North Pole. "That pup doesn't have enough sense to come in out of the cold," Sweetcakes said as she watched Bubba run through the snow.

"No sense. No sense," a short bulldog named Clyde said. Every evil villain has a sidekick, and Clyde was Sweetcakes's.

There always was something about

Sweetcakes that made all the hair on my back go rigid. "Bubba will come in when he's had enough fun," I said with a good mix of snarl.

Sweetcakes curled a lip to show her yellow eyetooth. "Normally, I'd make you regret what you just said," she growled.

I knew she could do it, too. After all, she didn't lose part of an ear in a fight by being dainty. I took a step back and my paw sank in snow.

Sweetcakes tossed her head and sniffed. "Today, you aren't worth the trouble," she said.

"Yeah, trouble," Clyde added.

Sweetcakes turned and trotted through the snow to the back door. Clyde struggled through the snow to catch up with her.

As soon as Sweetcakes barked, Fred Barkley swung open the door. Fred owned the school. He was also Sweetcakes's human. Fred was nice, but he could be clueless sometimes. After all, he thought Sweetcakes was the best dog in the world.

Fred scratched Sweetcakes's tattered ear and smiled. "What's the matter?" he asked. "You're not letting a little snow bother you, are you?"

Just then, Bubba took another flying leap across the yard. He slid on his tail. Unfortunately, he was going too fast.

"Watch out!" I howled as a warning.

Too late. Bubba, out of control, was heading straight for Fred. And Sweetcakes.

Sweetcakes barked a warning. She tried to hop out of Bubba's way. When she did, her paws hit a slippery spot and flew out from under her in four different directions. Sweetcakes sprawled on the ground just as Bubba crashed into her side.

I gulped. Blondie whimpered. Floyd covered his eyes with his beagle ears. Sweetcakes growled.

"You're such a cute pup," Fred said, ignoring Sweetcakes. Fred reached down and scooped up Bubba. Bubba turned into a bundle of wiggles as Fred scratched the pup's ears. "This snow is fun stuff, isn't it?" he asked Bubba. Bubba licked Fred's nose, his chin, his forehead, and was going for his ears when Fred

laughed and put Bubba back on the ground.

"Enjoy it while you can," Fred said. Then he turned to go back inside.

Bubba bounded across the yard and jumped in a pile of snow.

"That was a close call," Blondie said.

Floyd nodded. "I thought Sweetcakes would turn Bubba into a chew toy," he added.

Woodrow shook his head, dragging his ears across the deepening snow. "Sweetcakes would never misbehave in front of Fred. But Fred's not around now. Bubba better beware."

BUBBA'S WISH

Woodrow was right. I was sure of two things. Sweetcakes didn't like any dog to make a fool of her, and she didn't like any of us getting more attention from Fred than she got. Bubba had just done both.

Sweetcakes scrambled up from the snow and glared at Bubba. "That pup is more bothersome than a fleet of fleas," Sweetcakes growled.

"Yeah," Clyde said. "Fleas."

Bubba didn't hear her. He was too busy chasing Floyd. I chased Bubba and forgot

about Sweetcakes. Later Rhett, Scarlett, and I tossed snowballs. I was in the middle of building a snowcat with Blondie when the back door swung open again.

"Dogs!" Fred Barkley hollered. "Come inside!" Fred Barkley really cared about the dogs in his school. He wasn't about to let us get too cold.

The snow was falling so fast I hadn't noticed how deep it was. Snow was everywhere, and Blondie's face looked like a wet mop. "I'll be glad to get out of the cold," she said with a little shiver.

Woodrow knocked icicles from one of his droopy ears. "I've had enough of this," Woodrow told us. "Let's head for shelter."

"It looks like Bubba got his wish," Floyd added. "Snow, snow, and more snow."

Bubba? Where was Bubba? I looked out at the play yard. Bubba had just dived off the teeter-totter and was digging through the snow to get into one of the tunnels.

"Come on, Bubba," I howled. "Time to go in."

"Awww," Bubba whined. "I was just starting to have fun."

"You can have more fun tomorrow," Blondie told him. "But for now, it's inside for all of us. Our humans should be coming to get us soon."

We slowly made our way back to the back door of Barkley's School for Dogs.

"Hey! Wait for me," a tiny voice yipped.

We all froze—which wasn't hard considering the snow. I looked around and counted my buddies' noses. Woodrow, Blondie, Floyd, Bubba, Rhett, Scarlett, Sweetcakes, and Clyde. "Casanova!" I yelped. "Where's Casanova?"

"Over there," Blondie said, nudging me with her nose.

Huddled on the teeter-totter was Casanova. He looked very, very small sitting in a deep mound of snow.

"Hurry," I barked. "We're going inside where it's warm."

Casanova tried to jump down from his perch, but he couldn't get out of the snow.

"Oh, dear," Blondie cried. "He's so little and the snow is too deep."

I perked up my ears. This was a job for Jack, the Wonder Dog. "Wait here," I called over my tail as I bounded through the snow. Of course, Bubba didn't wait. Bubba hopped through the snow in my tracks.

Running in snow is much tougher than it looks. I was panting by the time I reached Casanova.

"I'm here to save you." I looped a tooth through his yellow sweater, being careful not to scrape skin, and lifted him clear of the snowdrift. Bubba and I made our way across the yard to the cheering yips of my friends.

Even Fred Barkley gave my head a pat and I stood up extra tall when he said, "Good dog." Then Fred scooped up Bubba and scratched his ears. "You're a good pup, too," he said.

I glanced at Sweetcakes to see if she had heard.

She had heard Fred, all right. And I could tell by the snarl on her face that she wasn't happy about it.

SOMETHING
TERRIBLE

As soon as I hit the indoor playroom, I shook my body all the way down to my tail. The warm inside air tingled my fur and I immediately yawned. It was time for a winter nap.

I wasn't the only one with that idea. A family of dachshunds already snoozed in the corner and Harry the Westie was sprawled in the middle of the floor. Rhett and Scarlett didn't seem tired. Come to think of it, they never were tired. They tossed a tennis ball back and forth.

Woodrow wasn't snoozing, either. He usually never passed up a napping opportunity, but now he sat with his nose against the window. I trotted over to see what was up.

Woodrow nodded when he saw me. His forehead was even more wrinkled than usual. "This is bad," he said. "Very bad."

What Woodrow said next sent chills running up and down my back. "Something terrible is going to happen."

I pressed my nose against the window to look outside. Snow pelted the window, and a gust of wind rattled the glass. "Don't be silly," I told Woodrow. "It's only snow."

Woodrow sighed and looked out the window again. "Just wait and see," he warned.

It is not in a Wonder Dog's nature to sit and wait. Instead, I curled up and snored. I dreamed my favorite dream. Maggie and I were running through the park. She laughed and threw a ball for me to chase. Suddenly, my dream turned bad because when I brought the ball back to her she was crying. "It's awful. So awful," my human cried. Giant tears dripped down her nose and landed on my forehead.

"Huh?" I gasped. "What?" I shook off her teardrops and ended up shaking myself right out of my dream.

There, standing over me, was Blondie. Woodrow and Floyd were huddled near her. Blondie was crying. Little teardrops gleamed on her white furry nose. "It's awful," she was saying. "So awful."

"I told you something bad was going to happen," Woodrow said with a nod that sent his ears dragging across the floor.

Floyd dropped the tennis ball in his mouth. "It's not awful at all. I think it's great."

"What?" I asked, scratching a paw on the tile floor. "What is going on?"

Blondie wiped away a tear with a delicate paw. "We have to spend the night here," she whined.

"It's growl-iffic!" Floyd said. "It'll be just like the sleepovers my human has. Maybe Fred will make buttered dog biscuits and show movies."

"Sleepover?" I asked, trying to figure out what Floyd was talking about.

"Don't you get it?" Blondie asked. "We're stranded. The snowstorm has turned into a bad blizzard, so our owners have to leave us here for the night. I know because I overheard Fred on the phone."

Woodrow nodded. "We're trapped."

BUBBA'S FAULT

"I hope Fred has enough kibble to go around," Floyd said.

I hopped up, my two paws on the windowsill, to look out into the yard. It was totally white. Snow hit the window like tiny frozen marbles. I had chill bumps from my pointy black nose to my shiny pink toenails. Wasn't it about time for Maggie to come home from school? "Maggie!" I barked. "Maggie, Maggie, Maggie!"

Blondie put her paws on the

windowsill. "Maggie is fine," she said. "All our humans are fine. Fred called them at home."

"Maggie isn't home," I told her. "She's at school."

Blondie shook her head. "Humans come home early during a storm like this. Maggie is safe and sound."

"But we're not," Woodrow said. "We're

stranded here at Barkley's School for Dogs."

I dropped back down to the floor. It didn't seem fair that humans got to stay at home during a snowstorm, but dogs had to stay at school. I wanted to be with Maggie, but I figured we should make the best of a bad situation. "Maybe it won't be so bad," I told my buddies. "It'll be an adventure."

No sooner were the words out of my mouth when our bad situation suddenly got worse. Sweetcakes marched across the floor and stopped right in the middle of the room. She lifted her snout and howled until every dog in the room was listening. "Where's that bothersome Bubba? This blizzard is all his fault."

"Yeah. Yeah. Bubba's fault," Clyde panted beside Sweetcakes.

For the first time that day, Bubba's tail stopped wagging.

Sweetcakes scared most of the dogs at the school plumb silly, but not Woodrow. Age made Woodrow brave. He stood up on his stubby legs and looked Sweetcakes in the eyes. "You leave that little pup alone," Woodrow said. "This blizzard isn't his fault."

"Bubba wished for snow," Sweetcakes said with a snarl. "Well, he got his wish, and now I'm stuck with all of you for the night. It's bad enough I have to put up with you during the day. Evening is my time with Fred. It's Bubba's fault and he has to pay for this."

I knew Sweetcakes was wrong. It was a Fido Fact that Bubba's wish hadn't caused this storm. I knew one thing, though. If wishes could come true, I would wish that every snowflake would disappear. Then I could go home where I belonged. With Maggie.

SLEEPOVER FUN

I wanted to snarl. I wanted to howl. I wanted to tie Sweetcakes's tail in a knot, but unfortunately it was way too short for knots.

Unlike me, Woodrow remained calm. "We're not any happier about this than you are," Woodrow told Sweetcakes.

"That's a Fido Fact," Floyd mumbled.

"Leave Bubba alone," Woodrow said, and I was surprised to hear a hint of a growl in his warning to Sweetcakes. He might not look like it, but Woodrow was

one of the bravest dogs at Barkley's. He stood up to Sweetcakes, and that took a lot of guts.

Sweetcakes curled a lip over one of her fangs and glared down her long nose at Woodrow. "Come on, Clyde," she said. "This mutt isn't worth our trouble."

"Not worth it," Clyde said with a nod of his heavy head. "Not worth it at all."

Clyde followed Sweetcakes to the other side of the room. "Whew," Blondie said. "That was a close call."

Bubba peered from his hiding place behind me. "Why is Sweetcakes mad at me?" he asked.

I gave Bubba a little nudge. "You didn't do a thing," I told him.

"Sweetcakes is just mean," Floyd added. "Don't listen to her."

"She wants to be alone," I explained.

"But why?" Bubba asked. "Isn't a snowstorm more fun when you share it with friends?"

"Of course it is," Blondie said. "Everything

is more fun with friends. Let's ignore Sweetcakes and have some sleepover fun."

Bubba didn't need to hear it twice. He bounded across the room to play tag with Casanova. After Casanova got tired, Bubba grabbed Floyd's tennis ball for a quick game of keep-away. Then Bubba snatched Rhett and Scarlett's chew toy from them. The sight tickled my funny bone—which is, of course, connected to my tail.

My tail, if I do say so myself, is truly something to behold. It's long and furry. Bubba must have thought it was fun to chase, too. He hunkered down. His little rump started twitching. Then, before you could say pain-in-the-puppy, that little fellow pounced.

What else could I do with puppy teeth sunk into my tail? I howled. "Aaaa-rrroooooooo!"

Did Bubba let go? Of course not. He's a puppy.

"AAAAA-RRROOOOOOOO!" I howled again as I tried to grab one of his ears.

I think Bubba held on even tighter.

This called for a Wonder Dog howl. "AAAAAAA-RRRRRROOOOOOO!"

Bubba didn't pay any attention to me, but somebody else did.

Sweetcakes.

No Picnic

"Stop all that racket!" Sweetcakes growled at Bubba and me. "How's a dog supposed to get any sleep around here?"

Bubba dropped my tail out of his mouth, which was a big relief to me. "Sorry, Sweetcakes," Bubba said. "I was just having a little fun."

Sweetcakes bared her teeth. "If it was up to me, I would've left you all out in the cold tonight."

"Not me, though," Clyde panted beside Sweetcakes. "Right?"

"All of you," Sweetcakes growled, showing one of her yellow choppers. "The only way I'll get any rest is to get rid of all of you."

Clyde whined and backed away from Sweetcakes. I felt a little sorry for Clyde. It must be tough to find out your best friend doesn't care if you get rolled into a giant snowball.

Floyd dropped the rubber reindeer he'd been chewing and looked up at Sweetcakes. "It's freezing out there. Surely you wouldn't kick a dog out into that snowstorm?"

"As long as I had enough kibble and a warm blanket, I wouldn't care who was out in the storm," Sweetcakes said. I knew she meant it, too. Sweetcakes only cared about one thing. Herself.

"All this dog fussing makes me tired," Woodrow said. "Let's get some rest."

"Woodrow is right," Floyd said, only it

sounded like "Woffrow id widt," because he was chewing on the reindeer again.

We all sniffed around and found good spots. I turned three times and settled down on a blue furry mat. Bubba snuggled in beside me, and Blondie found a rug spot not far away.

Everything was quite cozy until Fred spoiled it. He popped his head inside the door and yelled. "Okay, pups. Let's head outside for one more round of exercise."

Woodrow groaned. "Do we have to?" he mumbled from under a long floppy ear.

Fred seemed to understand dog-speak. He nodded his head. "Come on. One more time and then we'll call it a night." He held open the door and a blast of cold air rushed inside the room.

Casanova, Bubba, and Floyd bounded outside. The rest of us dogs followed slowly. We knew this exercise wasn't going to be a picnic in the park, and we weren't wrong.

GHOST STORY

The snow fell so fast the play yard looked like it was a giant fluffy pillow. Just the thought made me yawn. All I wanted to do was get back inside fast to get warm. Fred let us out for only a few minutes, but it seemed like a lifetime. By the time we got inside, everyone had frost on their nose and toes.

I had to laugh at Woodrow. His ears dragged on the ground and the bottoms were solid white. It looked like he had dipped his ears in white paint.

Shake. Shake. Roll. Roll. It was the same all over the big sleeping room. Dogs and pups rolled and shook to get dry.

"How about a late-night treat?" Fred asked.

No dog, no matter how calm or cool, can resist a treat. We all hopped around Fred like crazed Easter bunnies. "Treat! Treat!" Casanova whined.

A nice treat in my tummy was just the thing. Fred turned out the lights and I was ready to snooze. I found my blue mat again and was about to nod off when Floyd started talking. "When my humans have a sleepover they always tell ghost stories."

"G-g-g-ghost stories?" Blondie asked. "I'm not sure that's such a good idea."

Floyd barked. "Oh, it's great fun. The humans scream when it's over, and pull the covers over their heads."

"That doesn't sound like fun to me,"

Woodrow said as he put his head down.

"Humans are strange sometimes," Casanova grunted.

I had to agree. Sometimes my human Maggie did the strangest things. One time she gave me a whole ham sandwich, just because it fell on the floor. Let me tell you, a little dirt never hurt a good ham sandwich.

Floyd couldn't be stopped. He had to tell a ghost story. So he did.

"One night, a long time ago, there was a full moon. A pretty white poodle met this tall, handsome hound. They fell in love and married. The funny thing was, the hound would never take a bath. Now, the poodle was quite dainty, and soon the dirty hound smell bothered her. 'You have to take a bath,' she told him.

"The hound hung his head. 'I can't,' he told the poodle. But he refused to tell her why. One night, when there was another full moon, the poodle decided to take things into her own paws. She would give the hound a bath while he slept.

"Very quietly, she got warm water and shampoo. Then she set about taking off the hound's collar. It was old and rusty, for he never removed it. The poodle was almost ready to give up when the collar snapped off."

Floyd paused and the room was silent,

except for the snoring of a few dogs. Casanova squeaked, "Don't stop now. What happened next?"

"When the collar came off, the hound turned into a ghost dog. That collar was pure magic, keeping him alive," Floyd said.

Blondie gasped, and I scratched my neck just to make sure my collar was in its place.

"The poor poodle never got over the shock," Floyd continued. "And after that, she never took a bath again. If you ever run into a stinky, smelly poodle, you'll know that's the one."

I knew it was a made-up story, but now I didn't know if I could sleep. What if Blondie came over and tried to take my collar off? The whole thing gave me the shivers.

"That's a great story," Casanova told Floyd. "Tell us another one."

I shook my head. "No, it's time to be quiet. After all, Bubba's a young pup. I wouldn't want him to have nightmares."

"Good idea," Woodrow grunted. "Good night, Jack."

"Good night, Woodrow and Floyd. Good night, Blondie," I said.

"Good night, everyone," Blondie said.

"Good night, Jack," Casanova said.

"Good night, Casanova. Good night, Bubba," I said. There was silence. "Bubba?" I said.

I opened my eyes and looked around in the dark. The hair on the back of my neck stood up. Something was wrong. Where was Bubba?

BLIZZARD OF THE CENTURY

"Bubba's probably already asleep," Floyd said.

"Bubba?" I called. Still, he didn't answer. The only thing I heard was Clyde's snoring. I had a very bad feeling. "Find Bubba," I told all the dogs around me.

Let me tell you, we searched every inch of that sleeping room. Bubba simply wasn't there. "Fan out," I said sharply. "Check this whole school."

Without a word, dogs raced off to find

Bubba. In twenty minutes they were back. No Bubba.

"Where is he?" Blondie asked, sounding very worried.

I bounded over to the window to peer out. "Has anyone seen Bubba since we went out for exercise?" I asked.

All the dogs shook their heads. "Oh, my gosh," Blondie whined. "Bubba is out there in the blizzard of the century!"

"Maybe he's just hiding under one

of the blankets," Woodrow suggested.

I ran around the room tossing blankets, doggie beds, and rugs into the air. Bubba wasn't under any of them. Floyd nudged the sleeping dogs, just to make sure Bubba wasn't hiding behind them. No Bubba.

"Okay, everybody. Think," I said. "When was the last time you spoke to Bubba?"

Everyone was quiet for a minute, except for some toe licking. Floyd finally spoke up. "Bubba said he didn't want to be where he wasn't wanted. He knew Sweetcakes didn't want him here."

Sweetcakes stood up and shook. "The pup has that right. I don't want any of you here. This is my home."

Woodrow didn't waste any time. He waddled over to Sweetcakes and got nose to nose. "Listen here, Sweetcakes," Woodrow growled. "This isn't funny. If you know where Bubba is, you tell us. Now."

I closed my eyes. I didn't want to see Sweetcakes gobble up Woodrow. But it didn't happen. Sweetcakes sat down and scratched her ragged ear before answering. "Don't get your fleas all worked up. I don't know where that pup is now."

I didn't want to believe Sweetcakes, but I did. We all looked out the window into the play yard. That was the last place everyone had seen Bubba. I pressed my nose against the cold glass.

The snow fell so fast it looked like a white curtain. Blondie looked out the window beside me.

"Oh, Jack," Blondie moaned. "What are we going to do?"

I shivered. "I don't know how, but somehow I've got to get out in that blizzard and save Bubba."

BIG MISTAKE

I pressed my nose to the window. There was no sign of Bubba. But then the blowing snow was as thick as a cloud.

"Oh, Jack," Blondie whined. "Bubba must be scared."

"And cold," Floyd added.

I was a Wonder Dog. I had to do something. I pushed my nose against the window, trying to shove it up. It was locked tight. All I got was a bruised nose.

"Excuse me," Casanova said, coming up beside me.

"Not now," I told the tiny fellow. "I have a job to do."

I went to the door. It was closed tight. Maybe I could get Fred to come. I barked. Not just a little bark. A Wonder Dog bark. Then I waited. I waited a long time. No Fred.

Casanova hopped in front of me. "Jack, could I say something?"

"Later, Casanova," I told him. "I have to think."

I sat down to scratch and figure out what to do. Somehow, I had to get that door opened. I looked down at the tiny crack of carpet. A dog can do two things. Bark and dig. Maybe I could dig myself out. I pawed frantically at the carpet. I dug until my paws were stinging and my breath came in ragged pants. The only thing I got was a long piece of carpet stuck between my claws.

I plopped down, my nose jammed

against the door. I couldn't do it. There was no way out. Bubba might freeze to death and there was nothing I could do about it. I was so sad, I howled.

All of a sudden, a tiny little nose thrust itself in front of my eyes. It was Casanova. "Maybe I can help," he said.

"You?" I asked. "How could a tiny pup like you help?"

"I'm little," he said. "So I'm used to looking up."

I sighed. "It's nice to know you look up to me," I told the tiny guy. "But this isn't the time to talk about it."

Casanova shook his head. "I'm not talking about you. I'm talking about the door." To prove his point, Casanova looked straight up at the door handle. "I've watched Fred," he told me. "I think if I could reach that knob, I could open it."

I looked at Casanova with new respect. He was tiny, but he had a big brain.

"Hop on," I told Casanova, "and hang on tight." Casanova jumped on my back. Casanova crawled up my shoulders, then hopped on my head. He reached up and grabbed the door handle. I heard a tiny click and the door swung open.

"You did it!" Blondie yelped, rushing to my side.

We were hit by a cold blast of air. The snow whizzed around us like white fireflies gone berserk.

"This is where you get off," I told Casanova. "I'll go the rest of the way myself."

"How will you find Bubba?" he asked.

I peered through the falling snow. Wind blew back my ears and made my eyes tear up. The backyard seemed mighty big. It could take hours of digging through the snow.

I had no choice. Without answering Casanova, I braced myself against the wind and trudged ahead. All I saw was white. The trees looked like giant snow cones. Bushes were cotton balls. The grass was a giant cloud. With everything covered in snow, I didn't know which way to go. I tried to sniff my way, but all I got was a snout full of cold snow that made me sneeze. I admit I was worried. Even if I found Bubba, how would we find our way back to the school in the snow?

Giving up is not the way of a Wonder

Dog, but I must admit, I was feeling mighty shivery when all of a sudden Blondie appeared beside me.

"What are you doing out here?" I asked her.

"I can't let you go alone," she said, batting her long eyelashes to get the snow off them. "We'll find Bubba together."

My heart beat three times faster at her words, but I couldn't let Blondie get lost in the blizzard, too. I'm not too proud to admit when I've made a mistake. This time I'd made a big one. It was too dangerous to be running around in this kind of weather. Blondie and I could get lost. We'd probably be two frozen lumps in the snow.

"I'm sorry," I told Blondie. "This was a bad idea." I hung my head down. But that's when I came up with a Wonder Dog idea.

HEROES

"Your sweater!" I barked.

Blondie shrugged. "I know it looks silly, but my human made me wear it."

"It's perfect," I said. "It's just what we need." I grabbed a loose piece of blue yarn on Blondie's sweater and pulled.

"Are you crazy?" she shouted. "This is almost new."

"Sorry about that," I said, but I kept on pulling. "We need to leave a trail so we can find our way back."

Blondie nodded and helped me pull. Then we started off across the frozen ground, being sure to leave a yarn trail behind. We headed for the closest tunnel.

"Bubba!" I shouted, but there was no answer. We made it to the first tunnel and all we found inside was snow.

The snow continued to pelt us, and seeing was impossible. "I'm scared," Blondie said. I didn't want to tell her I was scared, too. In all my two years of life, I had never been in a storm like this one.

"We can't give up now," I told her. Blondie nodded. I saw icicles forming around her eyes. I worried that she might get sick out in this miserable weather. "Let's hurry!" I said, and we headed for a blue tunnel.

"Bubba!" Blondie howled. "Where are you?"

Blondie's howling wasn't half as beautiful as what we heard next. Blondie stopped and lifted her head. "Listen to that," she said.

I listened. There was no mistaking it. Bubba's howls floated through the snow. "Follow those howls!" I barked.

That's exactly what we did. We dashed around the teeter-totter and headed straight to one of the long tunnels. Snow was piled around the tunnel opening. Blondie and I frantically dug through the snow and suddenly a head poked out from inside the tunnel.

Bubba looked up at me, shivering in the cold. He grinned as soon as I appeared. "Jack!" he said. "I just wanted to stay and play a little longer. But then I couldn't find my way back to the school!"

I grinned at Bubba. "Never fear," I told him. "Wonder Dog is here."

Bubba's teeth chattered when I grabbed his sweater in my mouth. Very gently, I carried Bubba through the snow to the back door, following Blondie's yarn trail.

Casanova was waiting. So were Woodrow and Floyd. Even Sweetcakes poked her head out of bed.

"You did it!" Floyd cried when I placed Bubba down inside the building. "You're a hero."

I shook my head. "I couldn't have done it without Casanova and Blondie. They're the heroes."

Blondie batted her eyelashes. "There's

room for more than one hero at Barkley's."

Even though the snow continued to fall that night, I was nice and warm inside Barkley's. It helped that I had all my friends close by. I didn't even mind Sweetcakes's snoring—well, at least not *too* much.